SOMETHING HAIRY CAME DOWN THE STAIRS

BY DAI MORRIS

ILLUSTRATED BY
GARY MARSH

ACKNOWLEDGEMENTS

My sincere thanks to all who love and have loved and believed in me especially my Mum. Ella, Stewart, Amanda, Rebekah, Thomas, Charlie and Amber. Amy and John Rob and family. John and Sandra. Bob and Glenys, Lynne and Mark. Keil. Shout outs to Tom and Jenny for their encouragement. Karen and the Wharfers, Helen, Kez. Chris,Lucy and Dobbie. Mandy and Glen .Carol and Lauren. Freya for inspiration. Gary for his magnificence. Neil for his luminescence. James for audio wisdom. Dan for photographic smiles. The digital crew, JJ and Ross. Yana, Colin, Marsha and Cat. Irena and Ted, Tasha and Suzie for their friendship. Mark and Denise for being there, Dave and Viv for love and guidance. Dig and Liz, Helen and Sarah. John and Maria ,Cora and Joe. Martin and Sharon .India ,Robin and Holly.Ady for the coffee. Karen ,Harley and Richard. Jon W and family. Rob B. Martin, Annette, Archie and Euan. K from Sumeria. Rach and Henry. Gav and family, Andrew and family. Joan for healing hands Georgia Union -daughter. Jon and Laura, Turner and Syd. Dave C and family and Paul P the legend. Work Chris for support. Andy D for Inspiration , Matty and the gorgeous Ryan. All my current and former colleagues especially Deb(work neice) ,Craig,Anita,Claire,Dan,Nicolle,Laura, Pete,Mike and Mike and Vanessa I salute you. Malcom Bevan, John Goodwin and John Childs could better role models exist. Dave P who taught me so much.

All the musicians, writers, theatre and film practitioners for guiding me and keeping me sane-ish. All those involved in animal care and conservation keep fighting the good fight. My sincere thanks to Helen Cooper and all the team at Amazon for their patience, kindness,enthusiasm and hard work. Rob ,Michael and Paul. Dad, Grandma, Grandad and Uncle Pat thank you for the memories and love. Sandy, Connie, Skye and Billy extending loving paws across the Rainbow bridge and Rufus and Petra for dragging me through the forest.

DEDICATIONS

For Ella

ABOUT THE AUTHOR

Dai Morris. an educator of thirty-six years writes with flair and a vivid imagination. Throughout his career as a dramatist he has inspired thousands of students to develop creative ideas that are sophisticated and innovative. Being born and raised in the heart of Sherwood Forest, alongside his Welsh heritage, has greatly influenced Dai's life, his love of the great outdoors and preservation of nature. He's regularly seen walking his rescued German Shepherd and Collie through the forest.

His book is beautifully written in rhyming couplets stemming back to his years as a Shakespearian actor. The text throws up so many interesting questions for the reader. Who is the little girl? Where are the parents? Are the monsters real? So many ideas to fuel the reader's imagination.

One deep dark night I awoke from my sleep
drenched in sweat, wrapped tight in my sheets
My mind a jumble what could I have heard
to make me feel so alone and disturbed
Did I glimpse from the corner of my eye
shadows forming huge bats flying by
I asked myself as I lay there frozen
"Is this all real or am I just dozing"
Dad said that I should always be brave
face my fears and never be afraid
Did I have the courage to explore
the night-time house outside my door
I wasn't sure what I might find
but I hoped it would not be unkind

My heart was thumping as if it might burst
Wondering what adventures I might have first
but I stepped bravely onto the landing
expecting to glimpse something frightening

I walked so quietly heading down
moment to moment looking around
but silly me when I reached the hall
I couldn't see anything there at all

Then . . .

Something hairy came down the stairs
I think it stole my teddy bears
It held them tight against its fur
and seemed afraid when one went "**Grrrrrrr**"
It was very tall with eyes like moons
and seemed to be humming one of Dad's old tunes
Its feet were huge and tipped with claws
and sharp white teeth were in its jaws
but not for one second was I afraid
and I even laughed at the jokes it made.
When it bent down its tongue was red
and I reached out and stroked its head
It grinned at me and then it said
"Hurry up little girl time for bed"

But I couldn't sleep I was far too awake
and so my bed I would forsake
but when I looked around oh dearie me
I couldn't believe what I could see

Something scary was in the hall
Well it said it was scary but it wasn't at all
In fact to me it looked quite cute
dressed up to the nines (it was wearing Dad's suit)
It winked at me with its one golden eye flapped its wings singing a lullaby
It took my hands and we danced on the floor
then all out of breath I leaned on the door
I had danced through my fears but with thoughts left unsaid
it didn't feel right to go back to bed
With the door to the living room really close
then me standing beside it as light as a ghost
If I turn the door knob what will I find
I'm hoping it will not be malign

So I turned the knob and I walked in
but all I could hear was a terrible din
because . . .

Something lazy was in the lounge
stretched over our sofa wearing a frown
Switching channels with the T.V. remote
and crunching down crisps with its huge orange throat
The volume like thunder ever so loud
almost as if I was caught in a crowd
It asked me if I could order some pizza
"Cos I feel a bit hungry and I don't want to eat ya"
It then wafted some dust from its big smelly feet
and trimmed all its toenails like it was a treat.
A gallon of cola disappeared in a moment
sloshing about in its mouth like some great furry rodent
it just kept on eating not a bit underfed
so I turned around to go back to bed

but . . .

Strange noises were coming from the back of the house
In the room where I squealed when I trod on a louse
So I went up and I opened the door
I bet you can't guess what it was that I saw.

Something hungry stood in the kitchen
juggling pans while its tail was swishing.
Squishing and chopping, kneading and twitching.
I asked it to stop but it wasn't listening.
Its hundreds of hands moved in a blur
and while it worked I heard it purr.
It dropped some honey falling down from a shelf
just like the time when Dad did a belch
So loud they said you could hear it next door
and it blew our dog over (he rolled on the floor)
I've never seen anything eat so fast
when its mouth was wide open it looked so vast.
It gave a big shake from its toes to its head
saying run along little girl back to your bed

So I climbed back up the stairs, no sign of old hairy
meeting all the odd creatures was making me wary
When I felt the urge deep down below
Toilet. When you gotta go you gotta go.

There inside what should I find (can you guess?)

Something slippery went down the loo
then popped up again saying "**How do you do?**"
Polite for something that lived in a toilet
So I said "**Fine thanks**" so I didn't spoil it
With skin light and glistening bright as a bell
You hardly noticed the terrible smell
holding your nose and not getting too close
cos if you stood next to it then you'd be toast.
Dad always said you should pull the chain
so that's what I did but it popped up again!
Saying "**Are you trying to flush me, well that's very rude,
I never mentioned what you do with your food.
So I'm going to go now but take it as read
that I'm going to check that you go back to bed.**"

So I turned around to wash my hands
and there I saw something I don't quite understand.

Something slimy lay in the bath
its neck was long just like a Giraffe
Teeth like diamonds were in its snout
it swam a bit then flopped about
and water splashed onto my head
just like the time when Daddy said
that spiders lived under the bathroom rug
and he bent down and gave a tug
which made him fall into the water
and I laughed and laughed (well I am his daughter)
and so I smiled remembering Dad
and the slimy thing it seemed quite glad
it lifted a fin looked up and said
go on little girl time for bed.

All these encounters had left me confused
all of the creatures had seemed so amused
Then I suddenly thought I'll ask Dad what he thinks
So I went to his bedroom and before you could blink.
I'd opened the door and what do you think
was waiting there for me to discover . . .
(I felt like a spy deep undercover)

Something sleepy lay down by Dad's bed
It opened its eyes and raised its head
Then it rolled over and started to snore
and spread like a carpet all over the floor.
It filled so much space you could hardly get in
and I was quite glad that I was so thin.
I don't think it would be fair at all
to be squashed by a something against a wall
especially when bubbles popped out of its nose
then the silly thing cackled whilst striking a pose.
Now it seemed funny to have felt such dread
So when it snorted at me I walked back to bed.

But I paused near my bedroom what was that sound?
Is there something else creeping around
Munching on biscuits, drinking tea from a cup.
I looked all around and then I looked up . . .

Something large was in the loft
I didn't know it was there till I heard it cough
but when it moved the floorboards creaked
and I felt tears run down my cheek
because the loft has always frightened me
it's dark and creepy and you can't really see
but the large thing whispered "**don't be afraid
I don't know anyone quite so brave.**"
Then I shouted out **"How could you know
you can't possibly see me so far below"**
It said "**I know that you're beautiful, brilliant and strong
and I know that it's here that you really belong.
So look out for me when your'e next in the shed
now better get busy and run back to bed.**"

So I walked back to my bed through the night-time house
step by step as quiet as a mouse
and there as I looked at the top of the stairs
all lined up safe were my Teddy bears.
So I scooped them up under my arms
and carried them back where they couldn't be harmed.
I thought to myself what a night this has been
and I must be dreaming the craziest dream
Perhaps it's because of the cheese that I ate
the pieces I'd borrowed from off my Dad's plate.
Then as I fell asleep I noticed the glow
of hundreds of eyes and wouldn't you know
it was Hairy and friends they'd tucked me in tight.
I knew they would guard me the rest of the night.

Lightning Source UK Ltd.
Milton Keynes UK
UKHW052030030123
414789UK00002B/30